Bluebell

The Fairies of Therwen Wood

Coming Soon – Bluebell and the Great
Honeypot Robbery

Dedicated to Sapphire.
These are the further adventures of Bluebell,
her beloved tooth fairy.

Bluebell

The Fairies of Therwen Wood

Published in 2021

by Lost Tower Publications.

Bluebell

The Fairies of Therwen Wood

by P.J. Reed

illustrated by Emma Gribble

Lost Tower Publications

Hidden in the greening trees,
Watching through the leaves,
Woodland fairies laugh and play,
And giggle through the busy day.

Everywhere the happy fairies go,
They leave a golden, sunny glow,
If you see sparkles on the ground
You know a fairy has danced around.

CONTENTS

Bluebell 9

The Office 0f Wishes 23

The Travelling Tree 31

The Doves 39

Silvertoes 49

The Wish Seeker 57

Jerk Chicken 63

Maya 71

A Wish Not Granted 79

School 87

The Oak Tree 94

Chapter One
Bluebell

Bluebell woke up and smiled. She was now one of the wish fairies of Therwen Wood.

Her job was to grant wishes to boys and girls. She hoped to be asked to grant some really good wishes, like visiting a chocolate factory, or meeting pirates in the Caribbean.

Bluebell frowned and crossed her fingers, as she wished her new job would go well. She did not want to get in trouble again.

Once in training, she had been sent to grant a wish for a little boy called Peter.

He had been a very good boy helping his mother look after his new baby sister, and it was his fifth birthday, so the Office of Wishes had decided to grant Peter a wish. Peter had wished for a dragon. So, Bluebell had made a green Irish dragon appear in his bedroom.

Unfortunately, the wish had not gone well. Peter had really wanted a pet lizard and not an actual, living dragon.

The dragon had roared once and then his green cheeks and tummy had turned fiery red.

The boy had screamed and dived underneath his bed.

Bluebell had screamed and hidden behind the plastic dinosaur on his window ledge, as a stream of fire came out of the surprised dragon's mouth. A large black hole appeared in Peter's brand new dinosaur curtains. He had cried and Bluebell had felt very bad.

Madame Primrose, Bluebell's wish teacher had appeared in Peter's bedroom, wearing a fluffy pink dress

and a pair of fluffy pink slippers. Madame Primrose had sent the dragon back to its cave. Then, she had cast a memory spell on the little boy, so that he would forget all about the dragon.

Madame Primrose had shouted at Bluebell for being a silly fairy and granting bad wishes. Then she had vanished in a puff of pink smoke.

Bluebell shivered. Madame Primrose was a rather angry fairy teacher. The tip of her nose went bright red when she shouted, and it had gone even redder, when Bluebell had told her about it.

'I must remember not to grant any bad wishes today,' said Bluebell, as she lay in her conker shell bed. It was so warm and soft that she did not want to get up.

The sun shone through the windows of her little red and white spotted toadstool house. The flowers in the pots that lined her bedroom window opened their yellow petals, yawned, and danced in the sunlight. It was a lovely, hot, summery day.

Bluebell groaned and dragged herself out of bed. She could not be late. It was her first day as an official Therwen Wood wish fairy.

Bluebell went to her bathroom and touched the little white cloud which hung above the door. The cloud grew bigger and sparkled. Then the cloud started to rain. It was a lovely, warm, magical rain. Bluebell jumped under the cloud and the water ran over her.

On a shelf, under the bathroom window, was a row of coloured seashells. Each seashell had tiny arms and legs. When they saw Bluebell, they jumped up and down.

'Pick me! Pick me!' they all shouted.

'Now, now,' said Bluebell. 'Be careful or you will fall.'

It was too late.

The pink soap shell jumped too high and landed on its back. The water from the cloud had made the shelf slippery. The shell skidded across the shelf. The other soap shells stood up and cheered as the pink shell raced past them.

'Weee…' said the shell as it disappeared over the side of the shelf.

Bluebell grabbed the pink soap shell as it fell. 'You need to be more careful,' she scolded.

The little pink shell giggled and poked its tongue out at the fairy.

Bluebell shook her head. Soap shells were very naughty. She put the pink shell on her face cloth. The shell rubbed its hands over the cloth, making lots of pink bubbles. The bubbles began to fly around the bathroom. Soon the bathroom smelt of pink roses. Bluebell rubbed the bubbles over her face. Then she put the pink shell back on the shelf.

'Now, stay there, and behave,' she said firmly.

The shells nodded and waved goodbye as Bluebell turned off the cloud and got dressed.

Bluebell put on her prettiest blue dress. It was made from blue flower petals. Then she brushed her short, blue hair until it shone, and put on a pointed hat made from a tiny bluebell flower. Bluebell smiled. She was excited to start her new job.

Bluebell shut the door of her toadstool house and jumped into the sky. She opened her beautiful blue wings and flew across the wood, leaving a trail of shimmering, sparkly, blue glitter across the sky.

The morning sky was very busy. Fairies were flying to their tree offices. Big black and yellow bumble bees were carrying pots of honey to and from the Golden Hives. Below her, Bluebell could see the wood gnomes walking along the woodland paths, the bells on the ends of their long bobble hats swaying from side to side as they walked.

Therwen Wood was a very busy place.

It was too busy.

Bluebell wanted to go back to her old home in Flower Meadows. She missed seeing her friends, the meadow fairies who cleaned the flowers and polished the woodland trees. She missed seeing the little white mice as they played chase through the grasses, or squeaked happily as they stopped to snack on grass seeds, and the beautiful blue birds who sang in the branches of the Great Oak tree in the middle of the meadow. Flower Meadows was a very happy place. Even the Head Gnome of Flower Meadows smiled, and gnomes hardly ever smile.

Bluebell had loved living in Flower Meadows. However, the Therwen Office of Wishes needed a new fairy as lots of children were asking for wishes. Bluebell loved children and wanted to help grant wishes. So, she had moved to Therwen Wood to join the Office of Wishes. This was her first day at her new job and she did not want to be late. Bluebell flapped her wings very quickly and flew over the trees.

Suddenly, a pixie riding a beautiful white butterfly appeared. The pixie was talking to the butterfly, and not looking where he was going. They were heading straight for Bluebell.

'Watch out!' said Bluebell.

The pixie looked up and pulled on the butterfly's reins, but it was too late. They could not stop.

Quickly, Bluebell dived down. Her wing tips touched the grass as she sped over the path.

The pixie looked down at Bluebell and grinned at her. 'Sorry!' he yelled and flew over the treetops.

Bluebell waved back at him.

'Why don't you just watch where you are going?' said a cross voice.

Bluebell flapped her wings more slowly and hovered as she looked down

at the path. An angry gnome with a blue bobble hat was looking up at her. His wheelbarrow lay on its side on the floor, as a juicy red strawberry began to roll away down the path.

'I'm so sorry,' said Bluebell as she landed on the path.

'Let me help you pick another strawberry,' she said.

'No, just leave me alone!' the gnome said.

He began to puff loudly as he chased after the strawberry. The strawberry came to a stop, resting against a grey stone, on the edge of the path. The gnome picked the strawberry up with both hands and placed it back into his wheelbarrow. His white shirt was stained red with strawberry juice and was almost as red as the two spots which had appeared on his white face,

'We do not waste things here, fairy,' the gnome said crossly. 'It will make some tasty jam, even if it is a bit bruised and muddy. My wife makes the best jam in Therwen Wood.'

'Er... I'm sure she does,' said Bluebell. 'I really am very sorry.'

The gnome muttered and walked off.

Suddenly, all the bluebells in the wood started ringing.

'Oh snap!' Bluebell groaned. 'I'm going to be late!' She flapped her wings and raced over the woods.

Chapter Two
The Office of Wishes

The Office of Wishes was in the tall elm tree, on the edge of the woods. Bluebell landed and knocked on a secret door hidden within the folds of the tree trunk.

A dirty-looking gnome opened the door. His blue pointed hat had been pulled down so far, that it almost covered his fiery brown eyes. It was the gnome she had met in the woods.

'You again?' said the gnome in surprise. 'What do you want?'

'Hi, er… my name is Bluebell. I have just moved here from Flower Meadows to help grant wishes,' said Bluebell as she bowed politely to the gnome.

The gnome shook his head, and the bell on the end of his hat jingled.

'Well, here at the Office of Wishes we do things very, very quietly. Wishes must be granted in secret. You do not belong here. You are too loud and far too clumsy.'

'But I was sent here by Queen Winterberry. I cannot go back to Flower Meadows,' said Bluebell. She bit her lip as big blue tears began to fall from her eyes and splash onto the grass. Some of her tears fell onto the yellow daisies that grew around the base of the elm tree. Their petals turned blue and fell to the ground.

The gnome jumped back as another

big blue tear rolled down the fairy's face, fell onto a daisy, and splashed upwards onto his white trousers.

A large blue spot appeared on his white trousers.

'Stop crying! Stop crying... you are turning everything blue!' said the gnome in alarm. He looked down at his white shirt and trousers. They were covered in red and blue splodges.

'I look like I've been painting rainbows!' he said shaking his head. 'My wife will not be happy with me at all!'

Bluebell took a hanky from her dress pocket. She wiped the tears from her eyes. Then she tried to wipe the blue from the gnome's trousers. The blue tear stains mixed with the red strawberry stains and grew into an even bigger dark purple splodge.

'Get away from me!' the gnome screamed, as he tried to hide behind the door. 'Very well. You can come and work here on a trial basis but only if you promise to leave me alone and prove to me that you can grant good wishes.'

'Thank you so much!' said Bluebell. She went to give the gnome a hug.

He hid further behind the door.

'Er… sorry,' said Bluebell bowing to the gnome. 'Thank you so much for letting me join the wish fairies. I will do my best to be a good wish fairy.'

'Just remember you are only on trial. I need to see that you can grant wishes without flying too fast and crashing into things, or causing a mess, or exposing fairy magic to the human world,' said the gnome. He bowed and tried to shut the elm door.

'Er…. There is just one thing,' Bluebell said, putting her foot in the door to stop it from shutting.

'What now?' said the gnome, his worried face poking out from behind the door.

'Exactly how do I grant wishes?' said Bluebell.

The gnome tutted.

'You need to go to the Travelling

Tree; from there you can enter the human world to grant wishes. It doesn't have to be a big wish. Just show me that you can be a sensible fairy and do your job well!'

Bluebell rubbed the tears from her eyes and grinned.

'Thank you so much for giving me a chance. I will show you that I can be a good wish fairy. I will fly to the human world right away.'

Bluebell leapt high in the air and spread her wings. She almost flew into a bee carrying a pot of yellow honey for the fairy Queen's honey cake.

'I'm sorry!' Bluebell called over her shoulder as she flew into the woods.

The bee buzzed in alarm and fell on to its back, its wings flapping upside down. Pollen fell from the sky and covered the elm tree in yellow. The honey pot slipped from its black feet and flew towards the ground.

The door of the elm tree flew open, and the gnome ran out. He caught the pot before it smashed onto the path. Then sneezed as a shower of yellow pollen fell on to him. His purple splodged, once white clothes turned rather yellow.

'Oh, bother that fairy!' the gnome muttered, trying to shake the yellow pollen from his shirt.

The bee landed, and the gnome gave

her back the honey pot.

'Thank you,' she buzzed. Then she flew towards the fairy palace in the giant oak in the middle of Therwen Wood.

The gnome shook his head as he watched Bluebell fly away.

'That fairy will be nothing but trouble,' he grumbled.

Chapter Three
The Travelling Tree

The Travelling Tree stood at the very centre of Therwen Wood. It was very tall and had long, brown branches which reached up into the sky. The top of the tree was circled by a giant fluffy cloud. The cloud was full of magic dust and sparkled with the colours of the rainbow.

Each branch led to a different land.

Bluebell flew over to the giant yew tree and smiled. The whole tree hummed with the deep song of magic.

She landed on a twisted branch at the top of the elm tree. Bluebell walked along the branch towards the thick, brown tree trunk.

A stern-looking gnome, wearing a white shirt, red trousers, and a white, floppy hat, sat on a bumpy knot in the dark. brown wood. He had a feather in one hand and a piece of paper in the other.

'Welcome to the Travelling Tree, the Therwen Wood travel portal. Name!' he asked, not looking up from his paper. All Bluebell could see was the top of his white hat, which flopped over to one side, its bell hanging by his ears like an earring.

'B... Bluebell,' she stuttered as she watched the gnome write down her name.

'Department!' he shouted.

'Er... The Office of Wishes,' said Bluebell.

'Very well, take this.' The Travel Gnome handed Bluebell a small green bag. 'This will give you enough magic dust for twelve hours flying in the human land. You must come back before the dust runs out. Otherwise, you will be trapped there forever.' He looked up from his paper and stared at Bluebell through a pair of tiny glasses, which were propped up at the end of his pointed nose.

Bluebell nodded and slipped the bag over her shoulder.

'Hold out your hand then,' snapped the gnome.

Bluebell put her hand out and the gnome stamped a picture of an acorn on her hand.

'This will help you keep track of time. The acorn will wake up and warn you when you are running low on magic dust, and you must come back straight away. '

Bluebell thanked the gnome and made her way to the end of the narrow branch. The branch split in two and weaved around one another forming a wooden circle. Shiny green leaves fluttered around the circle. Bluebell puffed out her cheeks and wiped her clammy hands down the front of her blue dress. She did not like crossing through travel portals– it always made her stomach go upside down and that made her feel really sick.

Suddenly, the leaves crackled, and a pale green pixie stood up and yawned. He had no shoes on and was wearing a dark green tunic. On his head, he wore a crown of green leaves. His bright red hair poked up through the middle of the crown. He looked a bit like a red and green spiky hedgehog.

'Hello, Miss Fairy, can I see your travel stamp?' said the pixie.

Bluebell smiled and held out her hand. The pixie looked down at her hand and nodded.

'Very good, Miss Fairy,' said the pixie.

He pulled on a twig which hung down

in the middle of the circle of branches. The circle began to sparkle, as it filled with magic dust. Bluebell stretched out her hand to try to catch the sparkling lights. Then she heard someone giggling and felt a big push on her back.

Bluebell tumbled through the circle.

'Have a nice trip, fairy!' yelled the pixie, as he pulled the twig upwards, and the circle portal closed.

Chapter Four
The Doves

Bluebell found herself falling through a heavy grey sky.

Quickly, she flapped her wings and hovered just below a thick, bubbly cloud. Bluebell grinned. She had crossed over into the human land and this time she did not feel too sick. Perhaps she should try falling backwards through the circle every time she crossed over, she thought, as she looked down onto the human land.

Bluebell watched as people in tin cars drove on grey roads which criss-crossed all over the human land. She scratched her head. Bluebell could never understand why people just did not grow wings and fly everywhere. It was much more fun and did not make the nasty grey smoke which made the trees cough. The roofs of the houses below looked grey too. It must be very early, she thought. The sun was still slowly climbing up the sky and the beautiful garden flowers were still fast asleep.

Bluebell flew over the houses and nodded to a family of grey-collared doves as they flew past her.

'Good morning, Miss Fairy. Would you like to join us for some breakfast?' Mother Dove cooed.

'We're going to the kind old lady's

bird table,' her son chirped. 'She has the most delicious bird seed! I love the sunflower seeds,' he grinned as his tummy rumbled hungrily.

'That's very kind of you,' said Bluebell. 'But I need to find a wish to grant, or I will lose my new job.'

'Oh, you're a wish fairy! That's so exciting!' his younger sister beamed.

Suddenly, a grey shadow crossed beneath the cloud. Father Dove looked up at the cloud and cooed loudly. He stretched his wings as wide as they could go.

'Quick children! hide under my wings. An imp is coming!' he said.

The two dove children scooted under

his wings. Mother Dove flew in circles above her family, ready to peck at the imp if he came too near.

'What's the matter?' asked Bluebell.

'You must go quickly, my dear,' said Mother Dove. 'Last month the imps began to cross through their mountain portal and into the land of humans. They are searching for silver and precious stones. They even tried to steal the jewels from our collars.' Mother Dove

lifted her neck and showed Bluebell her beautiful silk collar. In the centre of the collar, was a shining moonstone.

'That's terrible!' said Bluebell as she watched the imp as it flew through the clouds. The imp spotted Bluebell and the doves. It flapped its grey wings and sped across the sky towards them.

'Quick!' said Father Dove. 'Hide under my wing, Miss Fairy or he will try to steal your magic dust.'

Bluebell gasped and clutched the bag of magic dust tightly to her chest.

'But without my magic dust I won't be able to get home!' Bluebell said as she looked up at the imp.

The dove children began to coo

quietly as they clung to the underside of their father's wing.

'That's very kind of you, Mr Dove, but I can look after myself. You protect your children and leave the imp to me!' she said.

'Very well,' Mr Dove cooed. 'I will get my children to safety. Good luck!'

'Good-bye Miss Fairy!' the dove children called, their fluffy grey heads peeking out from beneath their father's wings. 'We will save you some seed!'

'You are a very brave fairy,' called Mrs Dove, as they flew away to the shelter of the old woman's garden.

'Good luck and may the Fairy Queen protect you all!' Bluebell called back and waved goodbye to the dove family.

The imp dived through the sky and hovered just in front of Bluebell.

'Give me your magic dust and I won't hurt you,' hissed the grey imp. Bluebell could see his sharp, pointed teeth. She felt her tummy flutter, as if it were full of butterflies, but she was a very brave little fairy.

'If you want to steal my magic dust, you will have to come and take it from me!' Bluebell shouted. Her sapphire blue eyes flashed at the imp.

The imp swooped down. His pointed fingers stretched out to try to grab the bag of dust. His dark grey eyes fixed on the little bag.

Bluebell saw him reach towards her. Quickly, she flapped her wings backwards and jumped two metres away from him.

'Give me your magic dust!' the imp screamed.

Bluebell shook her head and leapt onto a nearby rain cloud. Her feet felt wet as they began to sink into the fluffy cloud. She did not have long before she fell straight through the little cloud. Bluebell grinned. The cloud was full of water. She flapped her wings together very quickly. A cloud of blue glitter fell from her wings. The grey cloud sparkled blue and began to grow. Then the cloud turned darker.

The sky rumbled. The imp looked up in alarm just as the rainwater began to pour over the top of the cloud. The water hit him in the face, and he squealed with rage.

He shook the water from his grey wings and glared at Bluebell.

'You've made me all wet... and blue!' shouted the imp as he looked down at his once grey trousers.

'Good!' said Bluebell. 'It serves you right for trying to steal my magic dust!' She flapped her wings together hard. The wings created a big gust of wind which caught the imp and tossed him high into the sky.

'I'll get you for this fairy!' shouted

the imp angrily as he peered down at her from the safety of a thick cloud.

'You can try!' Bluebell called back as she flew across the sky.

Chapter Five
Silvertoes

A silver streak whizzed across the grey sky.

The streak flew past Bluebell. She felt something touch her wings. It was so fast that it knocked Bluebell backwards. She fell onto a soft cloud. The cloud began to melt. Bluebell felt her legs fall through the cloud. She hoped no one was watching from the land below. Otherwise, it would look like she was wearing the cloud as a dress!

Quickly, she fluttered her wings and flew out of the cloud.

A shower of silver glitter fell on her,

and she sneezed as some went up her nose. Bluebell looked up and grinned as she shook the glitter from her wings.

There was only one fairy in the land who made silver glitter and was always in trouble with her Gnome Leader for flying too fast. It was her friend, Silvertoes, the silver fairy. Bluebell waved, and the little silver fairy waved back. The fairy dived through the air and landed next to Bluebell. Their wings touched, and a cloud of sparkly glitter fell to the ground.

The glitter woke the flowers that were sleeping in their gardens. The flowers yawned and opened their petals. The grey land below the fairies became a rainbow of colour as the flowers opened their petals and began to spread their colour magic across the grey streets.

'Oh dear! That did not go quite as planned!' the silver fairy said as she looked down at the houses below.

Bluebell looked down and giggled. Beautiful flowers were growing all over the houses and gardens below her.

'It looks so bright and er... flowerfull,' Bluebell whispered as she watched some sunflowers growing so tall, they tapped on the bedroom windows.

'Hello, Bluebell, I haven't seen you for ages' said the silver fairy as she bowed politely.

'Hi Silvertoes!' said Bluebell bowing too. 'No, after the accident I got moved to Therwen Wood. I'm now working in the Office of Wishes.

'That's so unfair,' said Silvertoes. 'It wasn't your fault the rainbow turned blue.'

Bluebell giggled. 'Yes, but a blue rainbow was rather strange, and I tried to mix the colours so carefully but everything I touch just turns blue! I think I am much safer granting wishes.'

'Yes, you are probably right!' Silvertoes laughed.

'So, what are you doing here?' Bluebell asked.

'I was meant to sprinkle some dust on

the tops of the hills over there to make them sparkle and to make the trees and flowers grow, but I think I have overdone it a bit,' Silvertoes said as she stared through her silver shoes at the flower-filled land below her.

'But everything looks so pretty now!' Bluebell said.

'Thank you,' said Silvertoes as she ran her fingers through her long silver hair. Then she frowned.

'What's the matter?' Bluebell asked.

'Oh snap, my hand is tingling,' said Silvertoes. She showed Bluebell her hand. The green acorn on the back of her hand had woken up and it was yawning.

'We must have spilt some magic dust when we touched wings! Oh dear! I am running out of dust. I must return to Flower Meadows at once,' the fairy frowned as she bowed again. Then with a flap of her big silver wings she flashed across the sky in a trail of glitter and disappeared.

Bluebell felt her hand begin to tingle. She closed her eyes and whispered 'Please no.'

She looked at her hand. A green acorn glowed on her hand. She stared at her hand as a cold feeling crept through her chest. She had used up most of her supply of magic dust. If she did not leave now, she would be stuck in the land of people forever. But if she went back to the fairy kingdom without granting a wish, she would lose her job and maybe even her wings.

Chapter Six
The Wish Seeker

A big blue tear rolled down Bluebell's face and fell onto the ice below. The ice steamed and melted. Immediately, a circle of bluebells sprung from the ground. They nodded at Bluebell. Bluebell nodded back at them and wiped the tears from her face. She was a brave and strong fairy. She would not go back to Therwen Wood without helping at least one little girl or boy.

Bluebell reached in her pocket and took out her Wish Seeker, a little silver acorn sitting in a little silver shell. Then she rubbed the top of the acorn and whispered, 'Show me a wish.' The acorn began to turn in its shell, slowly at first, and then faster and faster. There was a whirring sound and the acorn rose from the nutshell. It hovered in the air just above the shell. Then the acorn opened like the petals of a flower.

An arrow made from glowing magic dust rose from the acorn. The acorn closed itself up again and dropped back into its shell. Carefully, Bluebell put the silver acorn back in her pocket.

The arrow turned in a circle, leaving a swirl of blue glitter in the air. The arrow stopped turning. It had found a wish. Bluebell smiled and whispered, 'Show me the way.' Immediately, the arrow sped away through the clouds. Bluebell flapped her wings and flew after the arrow. The silver arrow was very fast. Bluebell panted as she tried to keep up

with the disappearing arrow. Her right arm began to tingle, and she looked at the acorn picture printed on her hand. The acorn had got up from its shell and was running up and down her arm in alarm. Her supply of magic dust was almost finished. Bluebell looked back over her shoulder; the portal tree was too far away. She would not make it back in time. Bluebell felt lots of butterflies begin to whizz around in her tummy and she began to feel very sick.

Bluebell flew into a passing fluffy cloud and sat down wondering what to do. The cloud was as soft as a marshmallow.

'Calm down,' Bluebell said to herself in a stern voice. 'You can work this out if you only believe in yourself.'

Bluebell closed her eyes. She felt the softness of the cloud beneath her fingers and felt the wind smoothing her face. Suddenly, the wind blew stronger, pushing the cloud across the sky. She tumbled forward, falling face first into the little cloud. Her lucky silver necklace jingled.

Bluebell grinned.

The necklace had been a present from Winterberry, the Fairy Queen of the Flower Meadows, and it was magic. On the end of the necklace was a tiny silver horseshoe pendant. The Queen had filled the horseshoe with magic dust gathered from the flowers of the white tulip tree. Queen Winterberry had told Bluebell that if ever she ran out of time in the human world, all she had to do was pour the dust over her arm, and the acorn would be reset.

Bluebell sat up. She took off her necklace and carefully poured the dust from the horseshoe over her arm. Instantly, the acorn stopped running about. It quickly shoved all the fallen magic dust into its mouth. Then the acorn yawned and walked back to its shell.

It was soon fast asleep.

Bluebell's arm stopped tingling and she breathed a sigh of relief. She would have time to grant the wish and return safely to fairy land after all.

Chapter Seven
Jerk Chicken

Bluebell looked at the streets below her. They loomed like grey shadows in the darkness as night fell. Suddenly, the magic arrow dived downwards towards a little row of houses. Bluebell punched the air in delight and flew through a sleeping cloud, across to the house, leaving a trail of blue glitter across the navy sky.

The arrow stopped outside a pretty pink house and wiggled its tail at Bluebell. The fairy waved goodbye to the magic arrow. The arrow disappeared in a puff of glitter. Bluebell saw a light coming from the back of the house. She followed the light and landed on the kitchen windowsill. In the kitchen, a couple were making dinner.

The man had a big smile on his face and hummed happily as he tossed some chicken in a bowl of red spices. A delicious sweet, hot, peppery smell came through the kitchen window. Bluebell's tummy rumbled hungrily. The man turned and put the chicken in a frying pan on top of the cooker. His shiny black hair hung down in dreadlocks almost touching his waist.

'I wish I had hair that long,' Bluebell whispered as she pulled at her short blue hair, hoping to make it grow longer.

'Hmm… that smells delicious love,' a kind looking blond woman came up and patted the man on the shoulder.

'Jerk chicken will put the smile back on our Maya's face in no time, Mary,' the man smiled as he stirred the hot tomato sauce.

Bluebell shook her head.

These people were not glowing amber. They had not cast a wish. She scratched her head and flew from the windowsill, hovering in the back garden. The tiny bells on her blue shoes jingled in the silence.

Suddenly, a yellow light switched on. It came from one of the bedrooms at the top of the house. The window opened and a little girl peered out. Bluebell flew up to the window.

'Hi! I'm Bluebell from the….' said Bluebell as she landed next to the window.

The girl did not see the little fairy and she slammed the window crossly.

Bluebell wobbled and tumbled backwards off the windowsill. She felt herself falling. A prickly rosebush loomed up at her through the darkness. Its green stem was covered in thick, sharp thorns. Quickly, she flapped her wings and stopped inches from the thorns.

Bluebell breathed a sigh of relief.

'Perhaps I've come to the wrong

house?' she wondered. Bluebell flew up to the bedroom window again and frowned as she saw the little girl stomp

across her bedroom. The little girl did not seem like she wanted help from anyone.

'Well, I had better make sure she is not the wish caster,' Bluebell decided. This was her first wish. If she went to the wrong house and the wish was not cast, the rather angry Lead Wish Gnome would send her straight back to Flower Meadows.

Bluebell reached inside her little fairy bag and pulled out her Dream Finder. The Dream Finder was a wooden twig covered in orange flowers.

The top of the twig had been twisted into a loop. Set into the loop was a tiny ice crystal. Bluebell puffed out her cheeks and blew onto the ice. The ice glowed with fairy magic, then melted into tiny bubbles. The bubbles poured out from the Dream Finder and flew towards the window. The bubbles bounced against the glass and then popped, showering the garden with magic dust.

The rosebush woke up.

Tiny green rosebuds grew along its thorny stems. The rosebuds burst open into red roses. Bluebell giggled and jumped down into a rose, bouncing on its soft petals. The rose smelt beautiful and flowery. Bluebell wiped her face on a rose petal. Yellow pollen stuck to her eyelashes and the tip of her nose. She looked a bit like a hungry bumble bee. Bluebell sneezed loudly.

Her body shook and the pollen fell to

the ground. Above her the whole room was glowing amber. A big wish from the heart had been cast there. She was in the right place. Bluebell smiled... and sneezed again.

Chapter Eight
Maya

Bluebell flew up towards the amber glow and peered through the bedroom window. The walls of the room were filled with posters. There were dragons flying across blue skies and magical castles built on clouds. By her bed was a small white bookcase, so full of books that they spilled onto the wooden floor. On top of the bookcase was a tall, wobbly pile of books.

Maya was obviously a very intelligent girl.

Maya stomped across her bedroom. Bluebell watched as she hovered just below the windowsill. Maya pulled a pretty yellow ribbon from her black, curly hair and threw it onto the bedroom floor.

Then she jumped onto her little bed. The old bed shook and groaned. A worn yellow teddy dived off the side of the bed. It landed face down with his long nose hidden in a fluffy yellow rug.

'Oh! I'm sorry, Mr Ted,' The girl said as she pulled her teddy back onto her bed. His red bowtie had come undone, and she carefully tied it back up.

'There, Mr Ted you look smart again,' Maya said as she propped her teddy back next to the purple dinosaur on her pillow.

'I'm not angry with you. I know it's not your fault we had to move to Heatherton, but I really hate it here. I wish we had never come'.

She lay on her bed and stared out of the window. It was grey and dark.

Autumn was coming, and night was falling earlier every day. She closed her eyes and whispered, 'I wish we could go back home to Cloverton.'

Maya sighed sadly, then she took her new *Knights of Kircus* comic from beneath her pillow and began to read.

Bluebell frowned. She checked the acorn on her arm. It had been a long flight and the acorn was beginning to wake up again. She was running out of magic dust. If she granted this wish quickly, she might have just enough dust to get back to fairyland.

Bluebell tapped on the window. The girl did not move. Bluebell sighed. Fairy

knocks are very quiet, and most humans cannot hear them, especially if they are busy reading. Bluebell grinned. She rubbed the silver, moonstone ring on her right hand. The stone glowed with the colours of a rainbow. When the magic stone was fully charged, she wriggled her fingers and the window shot open. A gust of wind blew through the bedroom. The little girl sat up, still holding her comic.

Bluebell flew towards her. The girl gasped, grabbed her teddy, and quickly hid under her duvet cover. Bluebell landed on the lump in the duvet and giggled.

'Hello, I'm Bluebell, I work in the Office of Wishes. I'm here to grant your wish.'

The duvet moved, and Bluebell fell backwards onto her bottom.

'Er… hello. I'm Maya. How do you do?' The girl replied politely as she peeked out from underneath the duvet.

'It's nice to meet you,' said Bluebell.

'What are you?' Maya asked. Her big, brown eyes staring up at Bluebell, 'And what are you doing in my bedroom?

'Er… I'm a fairy,' Bluebell answered as she flapped her wings and stood up on the bed, inches from Maya's face.

'Are you sure?' asked Maya. 'I thought fairies only existed in books.'

'Yes,' Bluebell nodded.' I've been a fairy all my life.'

'Hmm…,' said Maya. 'This is all very

interesting. I'm coming out now, don't move!'

Maya crawled out from her duvet, holding Mr Ted firmly by his back paws.

'I'm here to grant your wish.' Bluebell dipped her fingers in the bag of magic dust on her shoulder and glitter puffed everywhere. 'I can grant it now if you want?'

'Err... what wish was that?' Maya asked, her fingers twirling around the end of her shoulder length, black hair. 'The one where dinosaurs are still alive or being part of the Time Raiders gang?'

Bluebell frowned. She was sure that

the Lead Wish Gnome would be most unhappy if she filled the world with dinosaurs again. They were too big, and they ate everything.

'Err… you wished to go back to Cloverton,' Bluebell said.

'Oh that,' said Maya. 'That will never happen.'

Chapter Nine
A Wish Not Granted

Maya shook her head.

'We can't go back. Daddy lost his job in Cloverton. He found a new job, but it was hours away from our home, so Mummy said we had to move here. If we go back, Daddy will lose his job here,' Maya looked very sad.

'Don't you like it here?' asked Bluebell.

Maya shook her head. 'I don't have any friends here. The children at this school don't like me. They all laughed at me, and I never want to go to that horrible school again!'

Bluebell put her head to one side, 'So, do you want me to make the school disappear instead, then?'

Maya laughed. 'I don't think we should. I just wish they would like me more. They said I was odd and that I couldn't play with them.'

'You don't look very odd,' said Bluebell. 'My best friend Indigo always wins the prize for being the oddest fairy in Flower Meadows as she always wears stripy socks and spotty dresses. She has a crown and everything.'

'Do you have stripy socks?' Bluebell asked.

'Er… no,' Maya laughed. 'My socks are grey; it's our school uniform and I have never won a prize for being odd. In the human world, you don't win any prizes for being different.'

'Well, that sounds very sad and rather boring,' Bluebell decided, shaking her head. 'If you have to be the same as everyone, how can you be different and interesting?'

Maya laughed. 'I think I am quite different enough!'

'At my last school we played *Knights of Kircu*s every break. I was a warrior and had to fight the evil Time Raiders. Who are trying to take over the world and…;'

'Really! said Bluebell in alarm. 'I have never heard of the Time Raiders.

Are they very bad?'

Maya nodded. 'They have a machine that travels through time, and they go into the past to try to take over the world.'

Bluebell frowned and stared out of the window, checking to see if the Raiders were coming.

'Oh, don't worry. They are not real!' Maya laughed. 'It's all in here,' she said tapping her comic book.

Bluebell breathed a sigh of relief. She really did not fancy fighting time-travelling monsters.

'So anyway, yesterday at playtime I told everyone about the new game. Alice said it sounded silly. She said if I wanted to be her friend, I would have to sit on the bench and watch the boys play football. I said that sounded really boring and I'd much rather protect the world from Time Raiders every playtime.'

'That sounds much more fun,' Bluebell nodded.

'Well, then Alice told everyone that I was odd and now no one will play with me. Perhaps tomorrow I should just sit on a bench and become cooler,' Maya said solemnly.

Bluebell was shocked. She shook her head and the blue bells on the ends of her shoes jingled.

'Why would you want to be like

everyone else? That sounds awful and sitting on a bench getting cool sounds a bit chilly,' Bluebell decided shaking her blue hair.

'Why don't you go to school and find someone who likes you because you are a good person and not because you sit on a bench like everyone else. Humans are very strange indeed!' Bluebell declared as she danced across the cupboard.

'But what happens if no one will play with me?' Maya asked, her big brown eyes wide with fear.

Bluebell smiled. 'If you stay true to yourself, others will come and play with you because they like you being you, and not because you are pretending to be someone else.'

Maya thought for a moment and nodded. 'I am a brave warrior. I'm not going to be scared of Alice and her gang! The *Knights of Kircus* are scared of nothing!'

Maya yawned and lay back in her bed. 'Thank you, Bluebell fairy.'

Then she closed her eyes and went to sleep still clutching her comic.

Bluebell smiled and yawned. If she went to sleep now and used no more of her magic dust, she might have enough left to get back to Therwen Forest. She crossed her fingers and jumped into the half-open sock drawer and snuggled underneath a pair of furry yellows socks with a big hole for Maya's toe to peak out from, in case it got too hot.

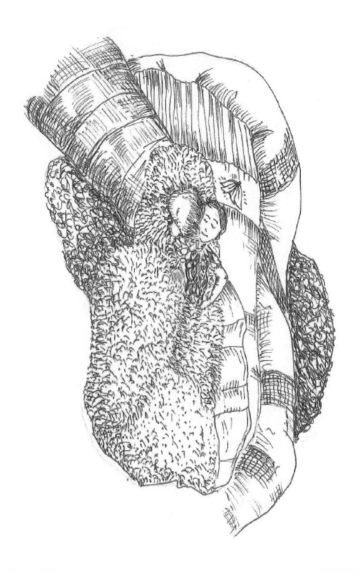

Chapter Ten
School

Bluebell awoke to an earthquake in the sock drawer as Maya rooted around to find a pair of socks that matched and rushed from the room. Bluebell sat up and pulled an old grey sports sock from her face. She sneezed and fell backwards into a pile of socks.

The front door slammed shut. Bluebell scrambled out of the drawer and flew downstairs. The front door was shut but being very small, Bluebell could fit into the tiniest spaces. She flew to the letterbox, but the box was shut tight.

Bluebell sighed and looked at her glowstone ring. The stone was white. It needed to be filled with magic dust again. She dipped her hand in her dust bag and the glowstone ring began to glow with magic. Then, Bluebell rubbed the ring and wriggled her fingers at the opening. Silently, the flap of the letterbox slowly opened, and Bluebell flew out. She whizzed down the road leaving behind a sparkling trail of fairy dust.

Ten minutes later, Maya's Mummy's car pulled into the school carpark and Maya jumped out with her school rucksack in one hand and a bagel in the other. Breakfast time was always a rush in Maya's house.

Maya kissed her Mummy goodbye and ran into the school playground.

Quickly, Bluebell flew after her. In the playground, she saw Maya talking to a group of girls all wearing the same grey uniforms, black shoes, and matching grey scrunchies. They looked very scary and rather bored. Bluebell flew over and landed on the black school railings.

'We are not playing your stupid game,' a tall girl said.

'You are really odd,' another girl said in between mouthfuls of doughnut.

'We don't like you!' the tall girl hissed at Maya. 'Come on, let's go and sit on our bench, before someone else tries to sit there.'

The gang of girls screamed and ran away from Maya.

Maya stood in the corner of the playground and looked very sad. Bluebell flew over and sat on Maya's head, 'Don't worry! I'm here with you,' she whispered into Maya's ear.

Maya jumped.

'Er, thanks... I thought you were just a dream! Can anyone else see you?' Maya sounded a little worried.

Bluebell giggled, 'No silly, I can only be seen by children who have made a wish from their heart – a heart wish.'

'Phew, that's ok then,' Maya grinned.

She re-tied her curly black hair with the yellow scrunchie, and it stood up at the back of her head. Then she took the latest *Knights of Kircus* comic from her rucksack and began to read.

Suddenly, a boy wandered over. The

frame of his glasses was held together with tape and there was a big hole in the knees of his grey trousers.

He smiled shyly at Maya.

'Um, hello, I'm Albert, is that the new issue? I haven't got it yet. We are fighting the Time Raiders in the mountains this break,' said Albert.

Albert pointed to the brightly coloured climbing frame which stood in the centre of the playground. 'Do you want to join us?'

'Yes please!' said Maya. 'I love fighting Time Raiders... and meeting fairies!' she grinned at Bluebell.

A head popped out of the climbing frame mountain and screamed, 'Quick Albert! The Raiders are coming!'

Maya and Albert raced over to the

mountain ready to defend the playground.

The tall girl glared after Maya. She wanted to play with Albert and his friends too but had never been invited.

Maya took a flying leap onto the climbing frame and waved at Bluebell. A big smile covered her face. Bluebell waved back and grinned. Maya was happy.

Sometimes happy endings happened without the use of fairy magic Bluebell thought as she flew up into the blue morning sky.

Chapter Eleven
The Oak Tree

Bluebell looked over her shoulder and grinned. Maya and Albert were sitting on the top of the climbing frame. The Raiders were nowhere to be seen but Bluebell hurried off just in case one arrived soon. She was pleased that Maya was happy and had made some real friends, but she did not feel very happy.

Her arm itched and her stomach had begun to ache. She had stayed in Heatherton for too long. If she did not get back to Therwen Wood soon, her magic dust would run out. Then the portal between the fairy world and the world of man would be closed and she would not be able to pass through. She would become trapped here forever.

Bluebell looked up at the sky. The sun was still climbing in the blue sky, as soon as it reached its morning seat, the travel portal would shut.

'I can make it,' Bluebell whispered to herself. She dug her hand into the bag of magic dust, but it was empty.

'Oh no!' Bluebell frowned as she peered inside the bag.

Something shimmered in the shadows from the corners of the bag. There was still some dust hidden in the seams of the bag. Bluebell grinned, there might be just enough dust left to get her home.

She tipped the whole bag over her head and shook it. A cloud of silvery dust fell all over Bluebell, covering her in silver sparkles. She opened her blue wings. The falling dust landed on her wings, and they shone in the morning sunlight.

Bluebell felt the magic enter her wings. She flapped them once and soared into the sky flying just above the soft, white clouds. Bluebell kept flying until she saw the branches of an enormous oak reaching up into the sky.

A ring of clouds circled the oak's thick trunk. It was a Portal Tree. Bluebell breathed a sigh of relief and landed on a long oak branch. She followed the branch until she reached a little circle made from twigs. Then she knocked politely on the tree branch and sat down with her legs dangling each side of the branch.

Suddenly, someone coughed, and the twig circle sparkled.

'Can I help you?' A pixie poked his head through the circle.

'Hello, I have just completed my mission and want to go back to fairy land, please,' Bluebell smiled.

'Hmm… I will have to get the boss,' the pixie said screwing his pointed face into a frown.

Bluebell began to get worried. She

drew her knees up to her chin and hugged her legs.

A minute passed. Then the grumpy Travel Gnome poked his head through the circle.

'You are almost late, young fairy, and you have used up all your magic dust. I will have to write a report about it.'

Suddenly, the sparkling magic inside the twig circle began to disappear and the gnome began to fade away. The portal was closing!

'Quick!' said the gnome. 'Your twelve hours are up! Take my hand before the circle closes.'

Bluebell grabbed his hand and the gnome yanked her through the circle.

They tumbled through the fairy sky and landed on the lawn in front of Travelling Tree. The landing was soft. Bluebell thought it very strange that the moss was so soft and even a bit warm. Then she looked down and found she was sitting on the gnome's round tummy. She quickly jumped off and apologised to the gnome.

The gnome stood up and dusted the grass, moss, and magic dust from his white coat. He put his hands on his hips and shook his head at Bluebell.

'Some fairies are almost as naughty as pixies!' he declared.

Then the lines dropped from his face, and he roared with laughter.

'Now go back to your toadstool and try to keep out of mischief! Tomorrow more wishes will come through and you need to be ready to catch them!'

Bluebell bowed and flew off to her little toadstool home. She loved her new job and could not wait to see what wishes she would grant tomorrow.

Lightning Source UK Ltd.
Milton Keynes UK
UKHW011259120921
390444UK00001B/22